THE INCREDIBLE HULK

Based on the stories by Marvel Comics
Adapted by Billy Wrecks
Illustrated by Patrick Spaziante

 A GOLDEN BOOK • NEW YORK

MARVEL

www.marvelkids.com
TM & © 2012 Marvel & Subs.

Published in the United States by Golden Books, an imprint of Random House Children's Books,
a division of Random House, Inc., 1745 Broadway, New York, NY 10019, and in Canada by Random House
of Canada Limited, Toronto. Golden Books, A Golden Book, A Little Golden Book, the G colophon,
and the distinctive gold spine are registered trademarks of Random House, Inc.

randomhouse.com/kids
Educators and librarians, for a variety of teaching tools, visit us at RHTeachersLibrarians.com
ISBN: 978-0-307-93194-8
Printed in the United States of America
10 9 8 7 6 5 4 3
Random House Children's Books supports the First Amendment and celebrates the right to read.

He's huge. He's green. And he's a hero who can smash anything. He's the Incredible

HULK!

When a scientist named Bruce Banner was accidentally bombarded with gamma rays . . .

... the powerful energy turned him into an incredible green-skinned giant—the Hulk!

ROAR!

Hulk is super strong, and almost nothing can hurt him.

The madder Hulk gets, the stronger he gets. No enemy is too big for him to tackle!

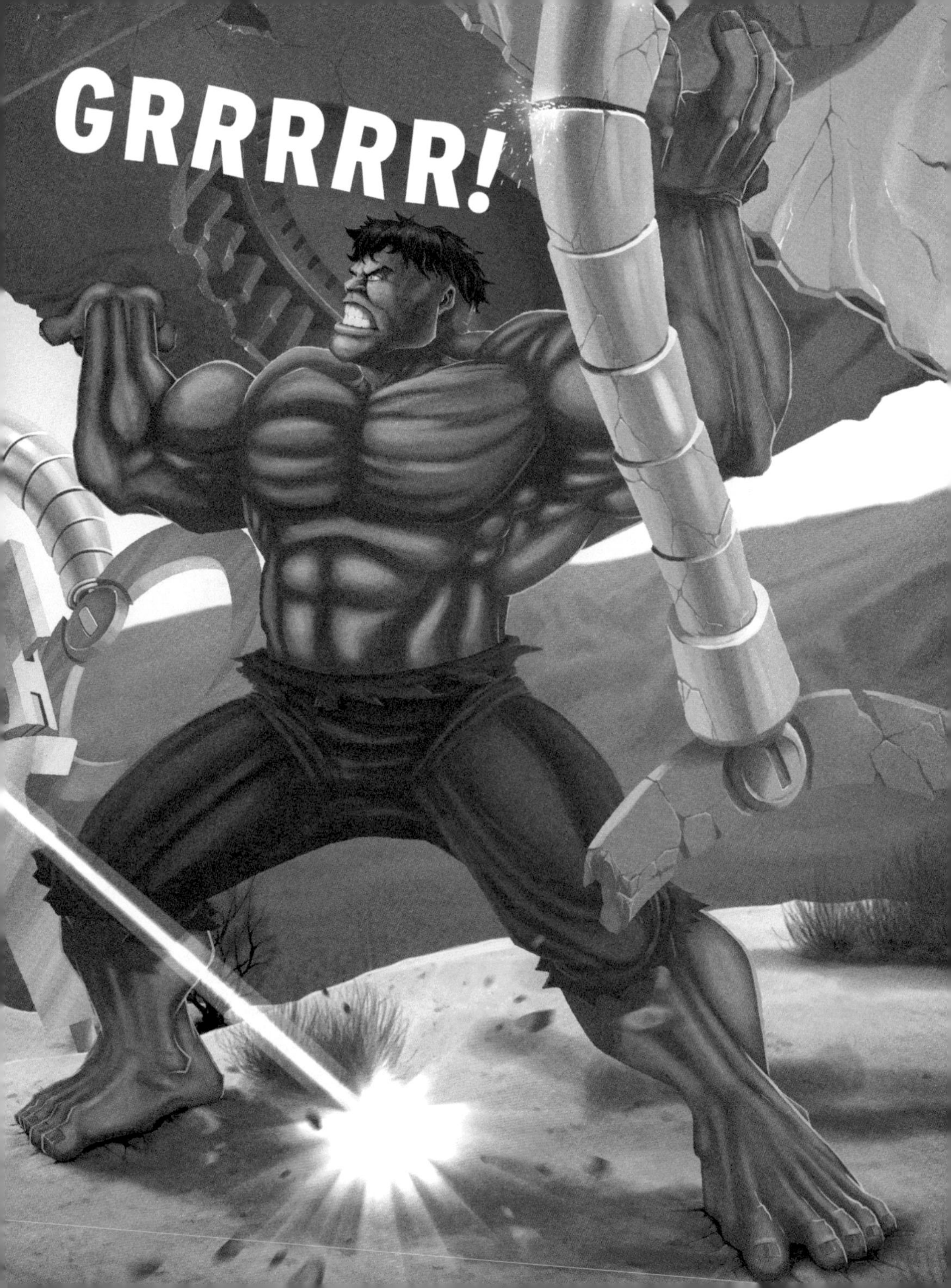
GRRRRRR!

Hulk can leap miles with his mighty leg muscles.

And he can create powerful sonic booms by clapping his hands together.

CRACK!

The Hulk is a hero, but some people, like General "Thunderbolt" Ross, think he is a monster. Ross wants to capture the Hulk—but he and the army can never hold Hulk for long!

Hulk faces many fearsome foes. . . .

Abomination is a scaly, gamma-powered monster who is as strong as the Hulk. **Rhino** has a sharp horn on his head that he uses to ram his enemies!

BOOM!

The **Leader** has a big mutated brain that makes him super smart. But instead of using his intelligence to help people, the Leader is always coming up with evil plans to take over the world!

Zzzax is a monster made of pure energy. This power-hungry creature wants to absorb the Hulk's life force to make itself invincible.

Absorbing Man is a thug with the ability to become anything he touches. He can be as slippery as a puddle of water or as strong as steel. But Absorbing Man is still no match for the Hulk!

No one has fun when the **Circus of Crime** comes to town. These performers use their astounding circus skills to break the law. But when they try to make the Hulk part of their act, he brings the big top down on them!

The Hulk also fights alongside other
Super Heroes, such as the **Avengers**. No matter
which foes they face, the Hulk is always ready
to help them save the world . . .

. . . and the Hulk always wins!

The Hulk is an incredible hero and a gentle giant.
Just don't make him angry!

Go, Hulk!